MW00874446

Summer Camp Survival

Tara Michener

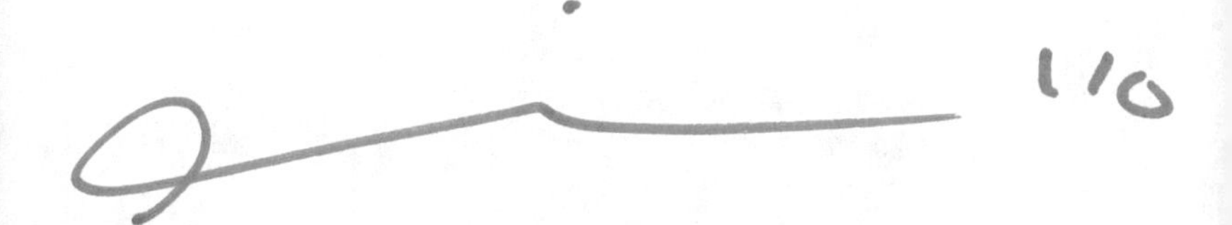

AuthorHouse™
1663 Liberty Drive
Bloomington, IN 47403
www.authorhouse.com
Phone: 1-800-839-8640

First published by AuthorHouse 8/24/2010

ISBN: 978-1-4520-6298-3 (e)
ISBN: 978-1-4520-6297-6 (sc)

Library of Congress Control Number: 2010911885

Printed in the United States of America
Bloomington, Indiana

This book is printed on acid-free paper.

Chapter 1

TWISTED SNARLS OF brownish-red hair flew into my mouth as I swung the heavy tennis racket at Tracey Blake. Tracey never needed to use as much concentrated effort to hit the lime green ball. Her neat black braids were placed in a perfect ponytail that flung itself beautifully as she passed the ball back to me with her brand new designer racket.

"Score!" she yelled arrogantly. I have no idea why I choose to torture myself by playing games with her. When the activity chart revealed she would be my tennis partner, I immediately felt nervous. She has been playing tennis since she was five with a private coach.

"Mackenzie Larson!" she screamed at me impatiently. "Hello...Seriously, are you even paying attention to me or not?"

I guess she gets special radar signals when the world stops revolving around her. Tracey Blake is one of the most beautiful girls at camp. She is very aware of it, and she wants everyone else to be as well. She brags often about her many beauty pageant crowns. She even brought them with her to summer camp and displayed them in her living quarters for all of her visitors to see. She is not one to accept anything or anyone taking attention away from her. I'm actually surprised that she does not wear the crowns to sports activity time to show off that she's athletic *and* pretty.

"Yeah, I'm doing okay," I called back with a pleasant voice, trying my best to focus on our tennis match.

"No...You are not doing okay! Your game needs a lot of work!" she snapped, with a bitter laugh.

My sweaty hands gripped the handle of my borrowed and tattered racket as best as I could. Tracey looked like she should be on a fashion model runway with her vibrant, crisp, white, designer tennis outfit, which contrasted beautifully with her smooth, brown skin. My second-hand tennis whites felt as though they were already yellowing from my efforts to keep up with Tracey's fierce serves. It was clear that my deodorant had quit on me and I hoped this fact was not obvious to Tracey, who smelled of sweet perfume. I'm not sure how she can look so pretty and smell so fresh after playing as competitively as she had for our entire match.

This resort is a place that many people would call a camp for the over-privileged. Don't worry, over-privileged does not describe me at all. Honestly, I do not even think people would consider me a privileged person. I am at this camp because I won a scholarship that qualified me to be able to come free of charge. I may be far from wealthy, but I am close to being a genius. Not that I'm boastful about being smart. I have actually tried to hide the fact that I'm gifted all of my life.

When I was in the third grade, I did my very best to fail every class so that the kids would like me and stop calling me a teacher's pet. It did not work out for me, though. My best attempts at failure in school garnered me an A- at best, and at my worst, I won awards for being the student of the month.

I've learned to accept that I am a smart person, I cannot change that, and I should be happy about my intelligence. My parents always try to convince me that being smart is a blessing, not a curse. They don't have to deal with the teasing and ridicule as much as I do, though. I know they tell me these things because they are proud of me and want me to be grateful for my talents.

Tracey's perfectly applied make-up glowed brightly as she walked away from the tennis net, and she began to pack up her name brand tennis gear in a name brand sports bag.

"I'm so incredibly bored!" she whined, looking at me as though I was the most pitiful person on the planet Earth. She tapped her foot methodically and said, "Mackenzie, let's call it a day...shall we?"

Her question was more of a statement. She looked at me and raised a perfectly arched eyebrow, daring me to disagree with her command.

"Sure Tracey, it's no problem," I said, with a tired attempt at a smile. "I'm actually very hungry and I'm thinking about stopping at the grill for a bacon double cheeseburger...would you like to come with me?"

"A bacon double cheeseburger?" Tracey glared at me and bared her pearly teeth. "Mackenzie, I'm sure that you can eat things like that, but I can't. You are already the most overweight girl at this year's camp, so no one notices when you overeat."

I was used to comments about my weight, but they were usually teasing. Tracey's voice sounded super polite, like she had asked me if I wanted a glass of fresh lemonade.

"You are so lucky!" she said shaking her head, causing her shiny black braids to sway side to side, agreeing that I was the fat cow of the camp. "Besides, I'm meeting up with my own friends to go to the mall and watch a movie." She was careful not to invite me along.

"Oh...will I see you later?" I asked, defeated.

Tracey was already on her bubble gum pink cell phone and ignored my question as she sauntered off in the opposite direction. As she gossiped loudly to one of her many friends, she appeared overjoyed to be out of my presence and into a conversation with people who really mattered. I stared after her, feeling utterly useless. The smell of my own perspiration was thick in the air, and the heat of the sun intensified the stench.

My thoughts turned back to the day my English teacher, Mrs. Cramer, announced that I had won my school's essay of the year contest. My classmates squirmed at the announcement that I had won yet another contest. I was very happy to win, but disappointed that my winning did not seem to make me any more attractive as a friend. I sat very still and tried not to smile, so no one would think I was being boastful

"Mackenzie, you did an excellent job and I hope that you enjoy your award."

Mrs. Cramer's gentle voice made me feel good for a second, until I heard someone whisper, "the nerd wins again," mixed with bitter laughter and more mumbling.

"Let's give Mackenzie a round of applause," Mrs. Cramer pleaded. I loved Mrs. Cramer, she always wanted us to be good sports and to celebrate the accomplishments of others. Mrs. Cramer handed me an over-sized, silver envelope that held a certificate with my name on it. The envelope also had a letter stating that I won the full scholarship to Camp Ellington. The brochures inside of the packet bragged about the state-of-the-art facility and the fun-filled days of planned activity and delicious food. The glossy brochure held the key to my happiness. I became enamored with the photos of kids who were my age having fun together. I stared at the pretty girls, who were possibly models, with tennis rackets in their hands. I pictured myself on the brochure. Wouldn't it be cool for me to be able to smile as big as those girls and have a fun summer eating great food and playing tennis? I imagined myself there, with tons of new friends and popularity. I blocked out the mean jeers of my classmates. I brightened with delight and a smile spread across my face. This would be my time to be with people who were friendly and fun. I would not have to endure the same old torture once I was at Camp Ellington.

"Boy, was I wrong." I said aloud, bringing my thoughts back to the present. I stood alone at the empty tennis courts, knowing the camp would never put this photo on their brochure next year.

Chapter 2

I BEGAN TO WALK back to my living quarters by myself. Yes, this camp has living quarters. I told you, it's not a real camp. It's a place where rich people get to go and pretend that they love the outdoors. They only spend time outside jogging in designer sweat suits or playing tennis. We don't live in tents or cabins. Our living quarters are like fancy hotel rooms on steroids. They have hot tubs and vanity tables, and a whole family could fit in the walk-in closet. My worn and weathered tennis shoes squeak on the floor and reveal that I don't really belong here.

I dropped my old-fashioned tennis gear on the plush carpeted floor, took off my dirty sneakers and flung my tired body on the bed's soft pillow top mattress. The silky comforter felt good against my exhausted body. My stomach rumbled noisily, reminding me that I had not had dinner yet. I decided to settle for a large bowl of cold sweetened cereal and milk from the camp cooler, which is really a stainless steel mini fridge. I crunched on the sweet taste of calories, smacking my lips and I caught a glimpse of my reflection in the over-sized mirror at the vanity table. The girl staring back at me with sad brown eyes made me feel very unhappy.

I racked my brain to figure out why it is so hard for me to make friends. Nothing came to mind, except that at school people always say I am the teacher's pet. But even at camp, without tests or term papers, I still have problems bonding with the girls. Their excuses are a combination of my financial status and my need for the scholarship. They notice that my clothes are not from this season, and they tell me so. Tracey mentioned that I am not as skinny as the other girls. Could that be the true reason why they don't like me? My brain raced with the need for answers.

I finished off the milk left in the bowl, slurping loudly. Wiping off my milk mustache, I watched my reflection thoughtfully. I have never been told that I am overweight, yet I can see that I am bigger than the other girls here. I am not chubby, but I am not a thin girl like Tracey either. I pinched the sides of my body, trying to see how much flesh gathered in my hands. No love handles, although I would never wear a shirt that revealed my belly button like Tracey often did. Her stomach was as flat as a pancake, and she never had a jiggle when she ran. I noticed that if I waved to someone, my arms would wave, too, with a small wiggling of flesh. I stretched out my arms and discovered that my tennis match did not give me instant muscle tone. My mom likes to call me curvy, and my dad says that I'm athletic. I guess the girl I see in the mirror is considered overweight, at least for this camp.

My brown eyes moved from my body to my head. My shoulder length coils had seen better days, and my hair looked wild and out of control. I ran a tired hand through the mess of tangles that refused to accept the styling gel I applied earlier in the day. The hardest thing for me about this luxury summer camp is that I am not able to get my hair styled on a regular basis. I was promised access to a full service salon free of charge for scholarship winners, but the stylist took one look at me and my crinkly hair and, with an intense frown, said,

"I do not do ethnic hair." Her thick accent sounded ethnic to me.

My face fell, and my heart sank. I knew that my hair was used to my two-week-cycle blow dry and flat-iron appointment with Tameka, the hair stylist from my neighborhood salon in Novingpond. No braids, no flat iron, no ethnic hair equals no luck for me. I don't always think of myself as ethnic...my mom is Black, and my dad is White, and we like to call my race "Bi-racial". Everyone at camp is very interesting, because they just call me "Black".

When I first met Tracey during the camp orientation party, she rushed over to me with a skeptical look in her brown eyes. She introduced herself and examined me closely with a narrowed glance, while twisting one of her long black braids. It reminded me of a licorice stick.

"Hey, I thought I knew all of the African-American girls here," she said, looking very offended that I did not send her a personal memo on my arrival.

"Actually, I'm Bi-racial. My mom is Black, but my dad is..."

"Whatever."

Tracey dismissed my words with her hand, revealing a perfect french manicure. She sucked her teeth.

"If you look Black, you are Black!" she said with a smile that did not reflect her words.

Tracey told me all of the girls with African-American hair made sure that they got their hair braided before they came to camp, so they could go swimming and have as much fun as everyone else. No one had told me I would have to take extra provisions to enjoy my scholarship award.

The phone blared and interrupted my thoughts. I picked up the old-fashioned princess style phone on my cream-colored night stand and answered. "Hello?".

"Baby, How are you?" My mom's gentle and soothing voice instantly made me feel better about my incredibly bad day. "Are you enjoying your camp stay, Honey?" she asked eagerly.

"It's okay...well, someone called me fat today with the biggest smile you could ever imagine," I shared sadly. Then, I asked, "Mom, do you think that I need to lose some weight?"

"Honey, you are the perfect size!" she exclaimed. "Don't let that bother you."

Believe it or not, my mom and my dad are my best support system. They always make me feel better when people say things to me that are mean or insensitive. Don't get me wrong, it's not that I tattle to them or anything like that, they just always know what to say and it makes me feel good that they care about my happiness. I always hear people at school complain about their parents, and it just makes me grateful that I don't have to complain or pull away from my family.

"Is Dad there?" I asked, pressing the receiver to my ear.

"Yep. He just came in from working on the car. One second," said Mom.

"Hey...how's the smartest girl in Novingpond?" my dad asked.

"Dad, I'm sure that I'm not the absolute smartest girl." I laughed as I rolled my brown eyes, afraid that I probably was the smartest girl in our little town.

Dad told me some stories about working on his car and how the garage looked better than ever. My dad owns his own auto performance shop and has always been a big car fanatic. He has more than one project vehicle and is always tinkering away under the hood of one of his many beater cars. He takes me and mom to old-fashioned car shows. My mom is a writer, and she works from our home. We always have tons of papers around the house because she never keeps her research in her private office. Sketches of children's book covers and page layouts can be found in any room in our home. She quit her job as a full-time journalist for a news program to work on books for kids.

My thoughts raced as I put the phone back into the cradle. I'm at a camp with over 100 girls 11 to 13 years old, around my own age, and I feel like my parents are my only friends. I stared back at the brace-face girl with the wild curly hair in the mirror and saw that she was staring back at me sadly with streams of tears racing down her light, copper-colored cheeks. She was so tempted to scream out of loneliness, but her mouth was silent.

Chapter 3

"Hello Mrs. Mackenzie," said the ultra perky, boisterous voice on the other end of the phone. "This is Janice from the main lobby. Your schedule for the day is at the front desk, and your activities leader, Lara, is waiting for you at the breakfast nook."

"Thanks, Janice," I said politely, then hung up the phone and rushed to get myself ready.

I brushed my bushy hair back as nicely as I could, but it still appeared matted and unkempt. Wispy strands were determined to escape the ponytail holder that I used to maintain my curly mane. I gave up on styling it when I realized that I was very late and holding the other girls up from their activities. I groaned loudly and tried to think positive. "I can make friends today. I know that I can," I vowed. I grabbed my over-sized purse and stole one more glance in the mirror.

"I've already won over Tracey," I said aloud, a lie I told myself.

I rushed downstairs to the main lobby. I loved the smooth, bronze, wooden furniture with soft, cream colored, cushions that filled the room. The grand chandelier that hung from the textured ceiling looked like it had a million little crystals in it that sparkled with intensity. My worn shoes and jeans always made me feel out of place. This room was built for someone like Tracey, but it had to settle for someone like me. My old shoes squeaked as I made my way to the smooth, porcelain counter and asked the cheery receptionist, Janice, who smelled of vanilla candles, for my schedule. Her plump hand tapped the counter.

"Name?" she asked. Her voice turned from cheery to annoyed, and she looked at me as though I might have made an error.

"I'm Mackenzie Larson. You just called me on the phone in my living quarters, like ten minutes ago... right?" I asked.

"Oh." She looked me up and down, from my battered tennis shoes to my frizzy hair. "Mrs. Mackenzie, this is your activities schedule for the day." She handed me a crisp sheet of grey linen paper with beautiful script outlining the rest of my day. It looked so nice, I was almost afraid to touch it.

The breakfast nook was in full swing by the time I made it there. Mixtures of laughter and various conversations flooded the room. The tables were divided into activity groups. Fifteen girls were assigned to each major activity leader. Our leader, Lara Phillips, plans our daily activities, accompanies us to and from activities and events and makes sure that we are supervised by an adult most of the time. She lives on the same floor as our living quarters. She is great at keeping us on schedule, but she never speaks up when people are being made fun of. Her skinny arms were folded defiantly, and she greeted me with an unwelcoming grunt as I entered the large breakfast nook. She was at the coffee bar with another activity leader, and they were immersed in their conversation about girls running out of shampoo and borrowing all of theirs. I groaned inwardly as I realized my activities leader had a friend, and I did not. I tried to smile and apologized as I passed them by and entered the empty food line. I realized that I was the last camper to come down to breakfast and was aware I needed to act fast before Lara called attention to my tardiness.

I quickly filled up my silver-plated dining tray with fluffy, buttermilk pancakes and a large pool of maple syrup, scrambled eggs and lots of crisp bacon. I squeezed in a cushioned seat at a table with my assigned activities group. I quickly began to pour myself a glass of fresh orange juice from the crystal pitcher on the table.

"Hey Mackenzie," Tracey said with an enormous smile that flashed gorgeous, pearly whites. I wondered if she got teeth whitening as I greeted her with a small nod.

"Hi Tracey," I replied, sipping my juice and a mouthful of pulp.

The other girls at the table giggled as if they were in on a secret. I focused on my food and tried to eat swiftly, so that my poor timing did not become a topic for Lara to scream about. As I was taking a bite of a crispy strip of peppered bacon, I heard my name being whispered at the other end of the long table. I ignored it and kept my eyes on my plate.

"Mackenzie is such a long name!" said Angelique Wallace, with a look in my direction. Angelique is a thin, pretty, blond-haired girl. "You look more like a Mac to me." She narrowed her eyes and stared at me. "Do you mind if I call you that?"

Her pale blue eyes turned icy and seemed to burn through my skin. She was daring me to tell her no. I truly did not like the name Mac. It sounded like it belonged to a truck driver with lots of facial hair, not a thirteen-year-old girl at a resort camp. I returned the stare that Angelique was giving me and decided to make an exception for her. If I wanted to make friends, I would have to compromise a bit. Besides, I thought, I've never had anyone give me a nickname before. I smiled at her.

"Well, sure. Can I call you Angie?" I asked, thinking that nicknames were the norm among the rich and fabulous.

Angelique wrinkled her thin, pointy nose at me. Her face contorted with disdain.

"No you cannot call me Angie!" annoyance rising in her pinched voice. "I look like an Angelique." She tilted her head thoughtfully and flipped some of her flaxen hair over her small shoulder.

She looked down at the diet soda, bottle of water and container of plain low fat yogurt on her meal tray, then looked back at me thoughtfully, took a sip of her diet soda through a straw and said,

"You look like your name is Mac and judging from your plate and how fast that you eat...I think I'll call you 'Big Mac'."

She laughed hysterically, and the girls at the table immediately joined in. Some of them laughed so hard that tears were running down their cheeks. Soon, laughter filled the whole room, and the joke was on me.

I felt my head drop as I realized that this would be worse than school, because at the end of the school day, I could go home to my parents and play video games or have chocolate ice cream. At the end of my camp days, I'm usually all alone in my living quarters with a bowl of cold cereal and hot tears.

I felt my eyes begin to sting and water and fought back the tears. I liked to reserve my crying episodes for my private room at the end of the day. I never wanted the girls to see me cry. I knew if they felt they could make me feel bad enough to cry, they would feel even better about making fun of me. I wanted to keep my hurt feelings to myself, so when I felt my lower lip begin to tremble uncontrollably, I said,

"Good one!" and flashed a weak smile at Angelique. I cleared my throat and politely announced, "I'll be right back, I think that I need to excuse myself and go to the bathroom."

The girls ignored me and continued to giggle in unison. I walked as fast as I could out of the breakfast nook and into the Ladies Room. I willed the waterworks to stay put until I got to the safety of the bathroom stall, and let my tears stream free once I was behind the fancy marble door. I thought, this is the nicest place that I have ever been in and the biggest prize I have ever won and I've never felt so alone in my entire life. Lara's loud, sharp voice interrupted my thoughts.

"Mackenzie Larson!"

I wiped my tears with pieces of toilet paper from the dispenser in the stall.

"We have been waiting on you forever!" she announced, so loudly that anyone in the bathroom could hear her. "I know that you did not pay for this trip, but others did and they want to get going!"

Her loud voice was stern and firm. Though her words were harsh, they would probably be the nicest I heard directed to me all day. At least she wanted me to join the rest of the group. I did my best to control my voice.

"Coming, Lara," I replied from behind my stall door. My voice cracked slightly.

I flushed the toilet, hoping she had not heard my sobs and walked to the fancy sink with my eyes down.

"Mackenzie, I am warning you not to waste my time." She pointed her bony finger at me with her free hand. The other was holding a travel mug that she clung to for dear life.

"Sorry," I answered simply. I lathered my hands and tried to focus on the suds created by the water and fancy soap.

I held back a few remaining tears and tried to focus my thoughts on things that made me happy. I wondered if my dad was working on cars today in his garage and if my mom was going to go to Tameka today for her wash, blow dry and curl. I imagined the scents of motor oil and fresh conditioner . I missed my two best friends so much. This was going to be a very long summer vacation.

Chapter 4

THE BEAUTIFULLY PRESENTED schedule of activities revealed we would visit the boys' camp quarters and practice something called networking. Networking is starting up conversations with people that you don't know and making small talk while you introduce yourself. The only networking I knew anything about was on the computer screen.

We walked into the boy's conference center as a group, but when I looked around the room, I noticed the gang of girls that I was with had immediately moved toward a crowd of boys, and I was the only one left alone. I began to look at my thumbs and anticipate my phone call home later that day. Sounds of conversation flooded the room.

"Hey, why are you sitting all by yourself?" asked a tall, attractive boy with caramel brown skin and hazel eyes.

His voice sounded friendly, and his smile matched. I was about to answer him when Tracey walked up, running her hand through her carefully braided hair.

"Oh are you talking about Mac?" she asked with a disgustingly sweet tone in her voice. "She's here on scholarship." Tracey beamed a flirtatious smile at the friendly boy, as she continued to play with her long black braids.

"Cool. Me, too," the boy said happily. He sat down next to me. "I'm Zachary Thomas, but my friends call me Zach."

He held out his hand to me. I smelled the fresh scent of soap and something else that I could not figure out. I looked at his outstretched hand and realized that was the first time anyone at camp had offered me a true token of kindness. I slowly took his hand and shook it, wondering if he would pull it away and say "just kidding" and call me a mean name. His hand was much larger than mine, and I felt calluses from hard work.

"I'm Mackenzie," I said quietly, being careful not to make eye contact.

He moved closer to me on the bench and ignored Tracey who was still standing near us, tapping her sandaled foot with a glimpse of her newest pedicure peeking out, waiting to be acknowledged. I silently said a thank you prayer, grateful that his gesture was genuine.

"Nice to meet you Mackenzie." Wow, I thought, no one ever told me that it was nice to meet me before.

The sentence swirled around in my head. Tracey rolled her light brown, doe eyes in disgust and quickly walked over to another boy to introduce herself and tell him about her many beauty crowns. I grinned shyly and listened eagerly as Zach told me all about his school. He was from North West Academy and played on the soccer team.

"I love it here...isn't it cool to stay in such a nice place with all of these cool people?" he asked, with a look of interest flickering in his eyes.

His tone was so warm and heartfelt. It made sense that someone like Zach would make so many friends; he is full of energy and plays sports well. I felt happy for him, but a bit sad for myself. While I agreed that this was a nice place to stay, I did not think that the people were very nice to me. Not wanting to bring the mood down, I did not share my thoughts with him. Now that someone finally wanted to spend some time with me without being forced to, I wanted to make the most of it.

Zach told me about his family and the fact that he was the youngest of three boys. He shared that his dad and mom divorced when he was three. He usually stays with his dad during vacations and breaks, but the camp has dominated most of his summer vacation time. I loved how honest and confident he was. He was very good at revealing his feelings without fear or being judged. I smiled as he continued to talk about the things that mattered most to him.

Lara's loud voice cut my conversation short with Zach.

"Young ladies, it's time for us to move along now and go to the next activity on the list...tennis." She read from the schedule in a monotone voice. "Please end your conversations as fast as you can and get ready to follow me in the next two minutes," she added sternly and without enthusiasm.

Lara's eyes stayed glued to her watch the whole time that she was speaking to the group. She looked irritated and that spread to her voice. One hand still gripped her gas station coffee travel mug.

My heart sank. I knew that it would be useless to ask Lara if we could have more networking time. I usually wished the camp activities would end as fast as possible, but for once, I wished this activity would last longer. I liked that someone at camp finally wanted to chat with me. It also did not hurt that the someone who was interested in talking to me had the most adorable hazel eyes that I have ever seen.

Zach also looked sad at the mention of our time ending, and he said, "Well Mackenzie, it was good talking to you today." He took out a ballpoint pen and a slip of white paper from his blue jean pocket. "Oh yeah, here is my phone number." He handed me the white slip of paper when he finished writing.

I felt a tingle of electricity as his hand brushed mine.

"I hope that you can call or text me soon, if you have time."

He smiled brightly, and his hazel eyes seemed to smile, too. My smile came... and went, as Lara yelled, "Mackenzie stop holding us up again!"

I noticed that I was the only girl still talking. The others were in a straight line behind Lara. She looked at me with exhaustion in her face and her hands on her small hips. The girls giggled meanly and glared, all except for Tracey.

"Big Mac...stop chatting, we need to go now," she called sweetly. Her cruel brown eyes narrowed and glared as her smile widened from ear to ear.

Chapter 5

By the end of the day, I was exhausted, and as I entered my living quarters, my stomach growled noisily. I was forced to play tennis with Angelique, who was even colder than Tracey. She called me Big Mac and hit the ball at me hard, as if she was trying to hurt me with it.

"I can't believe that you are so bad at tennis!" Angelique exclaimed.

The last serve she aimed my way guided the ball directly at my shoulder (I think that she was aiming at my face, but missed).

"Ouch!" I touched my now bruised shoulder and looked curiously at Angelique. Why would someone deliberately hit me with a tennis ball? Anger boiled in my stomach, and I tried to ignore it as Lara walked onto the court.

"What happened here?" she asked, looking from Angelique to me.

"I guess that my serve had more power than I expected," Angelique said with an apologetic look on her face. Then, she lied.

"I said that I'm sorry."

I was so upset. Verbal abuse was bad enough, but it needed to be clear to Angelique that it was unacceptable to hit me.

"Angelique, that hurt," I said, defending myself.

"She said she was sorry, Mackenzie." Lara told me to shrug it off and finally went to go get me an ice pack. She walked off of the court to go to the infirmary, and I rubbed my shoulder. Angelique shot me a satisfied look. I could not look at her, because the more I did, the angrier I became.

Lara jogged back to us. "Here," she said to me with no emotion or feeling about my sore shoulder. "Be more careful next time, ladies."

She plopped herself down on the side bench near the court. Angelique shot me a look of vindication while I held the freezing icepack to my shoulder.

The other girls continued to play tennis, but Angelique and I were told to sit it out for the rest of the day.

The girls in my activity group decided to go out for sushi, and considering I'm allergic to seafood (which they were aware of when they decided to go), I was left with another day of cold cereal with milk. I sat at the vanity table and looked at myself in the large mirror. For some reason, I always did this at the end of the day. My frizzed, curly hair was bigger than ever after our tennis hour, and my face was covered with a million beads of sweat. My shoulder ached from the day's tennis match. I waited for the tears, but they did not stream down my cheeks the way they usually did. My brown eyes refused to well up, and I did not cry at all. I found it interesting that the tears refused to come, even after Angelique's cheap shot during our tennis game.

My heart skipped a beat. This day was different, I thought, because I now have a friend. His name is Zach Thomas, he plays soccer and he's here on a scholarship, just like me. As I continued to stare at myself in the mirror, the weirdest thing happened. I smiled, revealing my braces and overbite. I even tried to ignore the constant ache from my shoulder.

I picked up the pretty princess phone and began to call my parents' phone number. I hung up the phone and picked it back up and dialed a different set of digits. I noticed the small print on the slip of paper Zach gave me had a happy face drawn on it, and I liked the way that the Z curved to begin the name of my new friend. I felt like my heartbeat got louder as the phone line started ringing. A male voice answered the call. I imagined the smell of fresh soap and the sight of hazel eyes.

"H'lo," the friendly voice answered.

"Hi Zach. This is Mackenzie."

I would give my parents a call later. I was happy that I had a friend my own age.

"It was nice to meet you today," I said happily.

Chapter 6

THE DAY AFTER I met Zach, Lara announced to our activity group that instead of playing tennis, we would go to the swimming pool for our fitness regimen. All of the girls screamed with delight and excitement, and I cringed with terror and fear. The pool and my hair do not mix well. I tried so hard to style my own hair. I borrowed flat irons from one of the girls and did my best to make my hair look the way it did when Tameka styled it. It was not as pretty as a professional's creation, but some of the girls even said it looked nice, and they never said anything nice to me…EVER!

I ran my hands through my silky straight hair and knew that would probably only last for another ten minutes. I felt my eyes stinging with tears. We were also going to have our lunch with the boys' camp, and Zach and I were planning on sitting together. I knew that he would never want to be seen with me if my hair touched the water and chlorine.

"Are you crying?" Tracey asked with the biggest smile I have ever seen. "You should be happy to go to the pool. Your tennis game is awful. Maybe it's that ancient racket that you got from the cave man museum!"

Tracey's joke was funny to everybody except me. She crossed her arms and happily shook her braids. I tried to stop weeping, but it was hopeless, and all of the girls looked to see my own personal water works display. I frantically tried wiping the tears away, but it was no use. They kept coming down as though they were attached to a sprinkler system. I was so mad at myself. Letting the girls see my tears was the last thing I needed.

Lara took me by the hand and led me away from the girls. Her blond side ponytail brushed her shoulder as her green eyes met mine.

"Mackenzie, what's wrong?" she whispered.

I noticed that her eyes had bags underneath them. Either she was older than she looked, or she was just really tired. She seemed like she cared, so I wiped my eyes and said,

"My hair....Can I skip the pool?" My brown eyes met her jade ones, and I noticed that the caring was replaced with anger.

"You mean to tell me you are crying over your hair?" she bellowed. "I thought some of the girls showed a shallow side but this is the worst yet!" Lara's eyes crossed with annoyance, and she took a quick sip from her ever-present coffee mug. "Mackenzie, don't waste my time!" Lara walked quickly away, with fast strides and frowning brows.

"Girls, once again, little Ms. Mackenzie has made us late. Let's get to the swimming pool!" she shouted.

Sneers from the girls followed me all the way to the locker room. I truly felt isolated and realized that once Zach saw me after swimming, I would truly be alone.

I squeezed into my plain black one piece. The suit seemed tighter than it used to be. It seemed to hug my body in all of the wrong places, and I felt inferior as I noticed the other girls in their designer fashions. Tracey looked like she stepped off of a magazine cover with her lily white one-piece. Her dark brown skin glowed, and her flat belly looked leaner than ever. I attempted to suck in my own slight pouch of flesh. Why did I have to have a mini-pot belly in the midst of all of these model thin frames?

We were not in for a leisurely day at the pool. Lara said that we needed to practice our pool safety to ensure that we met camp guidelines and that we were prepared for emergencies. We had to demonstrate the dead man's float, the back float and the jelly fish float before we were allowed out of the pool. I heard the girls laugh as my unruly hair swelled from my straightened flat iron effort to a jumbo, spiral afro in a matter of minutes. I held back salty tears and felt like I was choking on chemically treated water. I was the last one out of the pool, and Lara announced that, once again, I had wasted every one's time, and we would not be able to primp for long before going to the boy's camp for lunch.

Once we were in the locker room, Tracey and the rest of the girls talked about me as though I was not present.

"She is such a crybaby dork," said a short girl with freckles named Valentina Smith.

Tracey smiled at Valentina and said loudly,

"That's why they should not let poor people into camp." She looked right at me. My eyes lowered, but hers did not.

"Mackenzie, you know it's true." She tried to sound sympathetic. She grabbed a handful of her own braided hair. "You are so lucky to be here. That's all I'm saying." Her sugary sweet voice made me cringe with nausea.

Chapter 7

Although most of the girls secretly applied their flavored lip gloss and bright eye shadow when Lara was not looking, I did not. My face looked ashy. It felt dry from the pool water, and my hair was left completely untamed. I did not bring a ponytail holder, and no one would lend me one, so I was not able to pull my hair back. I entered the boys' lunch quarters and kept my head down the whole time, studying my battered shoes and wondering when my parents would let me get a new pair. I felt a rough hand on my shoulder, and when I looked up, I saw Zach smiling at me. He had walked over to where I was standing and welcomed me.

"Hey Mackenzie! I saved you a seat at the table in the middle." He led me to a table that already had two box lunches on it. "Do you like turkey or ham sandwiches?" he asked. "I grabbed one of each, and the one that you don't want can be mine." I smiled weakly, surprised at his kindness.

"I'll take turkey," I offered. The camp had our lunch catered from a trendy deli. The box included a sandwich, an apple and a bottle of spring water. We both happily munched on our prepared meals.

He seemed not to notice my larger than ever hair and my dry face. We talked about his soccer team and the activities that the boys' camp had participated in earlier in the day. I listened intently, enjoying his friendly voice and conversation. He looked at me with a question in his eyes.

"What do you like to do?" he asked, with a curious smile.

I was stunned. I thought we would just focus on his likes and dislikes in our conversations. I did not expect to talk about my life at all. I was flattered that he cared about my interests. I grinned, hoping that pieces of my sandwich were not stuck in my braces. I usually have that problem with lettuce. I took a deep breath.

"Well, I like to draw sometimes," I said with a smirk.

"Cool!" he responded. "Are you any good at it?"

"Yeah, I think so. I'm in advanced drawing at school, and they only allow the people that can draw really well to be in that class."

"I had no idea." Zach's eyes brightened. "How great is that?" He seemed to think to himself for a minute. His eyebrows raised and he asked, "Could you draw me?"

The way that he asked reminded me of a little kid asking for candy. It was so cute! I smiled, and giggled softly.

"Sure."

I studied his brown skin and hazel eyes. I took out my sketch book and drew him as a caricature. I was sure to add a soccer ball, to show his true character.

"Are you almost finished?" he asked many times as I was finishing up the lines in his drawing.

"Almost...be patient," I teased.

"I just want to see it," he started, and before he could finish, I turned the sketch pad around to reveal the drawing. His eyes widened, and he laughed with delight. He even called over some of his friends to view my handiwork. Lots of boys surrounded us, and they all laughed and told me that I was really cool and that they wished that they could draw like me.

The girls looked over with puzzled glances and tried to keep their cool while their partners walked away and crowded around me and Zach. Angelique and Tracey whispered to each other, but tried to remain unfazed by the obvious change in the room. Tracey looked as though she would surely pull one of her braids out. She cleared her throat loudly and stared at the boy who had been sitting next to her before he was called over to our table.

Finally, she had enough of being upstaged. She let go of her tortured braid, smoothed her pretty sundress with her manicured hand and slowly stood up. Tracey walked to our crowded table, smiling like she was the queen of the world. She looked at the sketch and gave an uninterested laugh. She beckoned with her eyes to her networking partner, Mike, who seemed not to notice. He asked me how long had I been drawing. Clearly frustrated, she gave a dry smile and asked,

"Did you know that she is only here because she is on a scholarship?" She did not wait for the boys to answer, but continued, "Her parents could not afford to send her here!" Tracey smiled with glee, hoping the boys would dismiss my talent due to my financial status.

The boys did not seem to hear her, so she said it again, even louder this time.

"I said...she is only here because she is on scholarship!"

I would not have been surprised if she had pulled out one of her many beauty crowns and told them, "I'm talented too. Look at me!" Many of the boys ignored Tracey and kept asking me about drawing and if I could teach them. One of the boys finally laughed and said to her,

"We all heard you the first time that you said it." He looked annoyed and unappreciative of the interruption as he mumbled, "I thought everyone here was on a scholarship. I would never want my parents to spend this much money on a camp."

The guys laughed and nodded in agreement. They stayed fixated on my sketch book and continued to ask questions. Some of them told me they liked to draw too and asked if I'd ever want to see their drawings.

The girls looked defeated, and Tracey sucked in her breath and slowly walked back to her seat. She sat alone, twisting one of her long braids. Her networking buddy, Mike, was still sitting with me and Zach, and still talking about the drawing I created. I felt her anger boiling from across the room but decided to focus on the positive attention I was getting from the boys.

Chapter 8

LOOKING AT MY reflection tonight, I see a new girl staring back at me. She has big hair and big eyes and a big heart. Not only is she the perfect size and pretty...she is smart. It has been a while since my mirror gazing at night brought tears to my eyes, and I am grateful for the new friendship with Zach. I realize that I don't have to hide my talent or intelligence anymore. No one cares if my hair is big and unruly at times. They still like me. I glance up and say a thank you prayer.

The phone rang loudly.

"Hey...Sweetie!" My dad's loud voice echoes into the phone. "I missed you! You have not called me or your mom all week." He sounded sad.

"I'm sorry Dad," I said, picturing his oil-laden hands holding on to the phone. "I actually made a friend!" I shared my news with him.

"That's great honey!" I heard murmurs in the background. "Your mom wants to talk to you too."

My mom got on the line, and I told her about Zach and what happened with the girls.

When she spoke, I could hear the smile in her voice, and I immediately missed her.

"Don't those people know anything about diversity?" she asked. "No one better ask me to put my head into a pool after it was flat ironed." She giggled, and I joined her. "So...do you like this Zach?" she questioned.

I was amazed at her question. I never had a real crush before. No one at school ever paid me any attention, and I reserved my crushes for movie stars and people on television.

"Well, I don't know" I said thoughtfully. "I'm just glad to have a real friend."

"You are so smart!" Mom said cheerfully. "That's my girl!"

Chapter 9

LARA ANNOUNCED TO us at the breakfast nook that our activity group would be going to the local shopping mall, and afterward, taking a trip to the local amusement park. The girls flashed toothy grins and made whoops of excitement. Lara told us this was a special treat, and she wanted us to be surprised, which is why she did not announce it earlier. I immediately felt sick to my stomach. I did not have any money with me because the scholarship letter explained the camp was "all expenses paid". The brochure or letter never mentioned any shopping trip or amusement park.

I raised my hand slightly, and Lara beckoned me to speak with a hand gesture. I exhaled with embarrassment.

"Lara, if a person is on scholarship, does the camp pay for the mall expenses and park fees?" I asked sheepishly.

The girls immediately gasped, and laughter soon followed. Lara looked at me in disbelief and put her hand on her head. She held tightly to her travel mug with the other hand.

"Mackenzie, the camp won't pay for you to shop and go to a amusement park." She looked at me like I was an idiot. "Didn't you bring any spending money?"

All eyes were glued to my reddening face. They wanted to see my reaction and hear my answer. I had no idea how to respond to Lara's question.

My parents attempted to give me some cash when they dropped me off. I told them that I would be fine. After all, the camp was all expenses paid.

I felt my eyes droop, and I shook my head as I met Lara's tired and exasperated stare. She took a deep breath and looked perplexed. The girls began to whisper, rudely.

"Whose parents would send them somewhere without money?" one girl sneered.

I hated them saying mean things about my family.

"Mackenzie, it's not fair to the other girls for me to cancel the trip due to your lack of money." Lara looked exhausted. "I guess if you want anything at the mall...I'll have to buy it," she stated with regret. "I'll pay for your amusement park trip and fees too." Her offer was generous, but she looked uncomfortable.

I heard Tracey whisper, "Charity case!" and looked over to see her cruel smile.

My eyes stayed focused on the shiny floor of the mall during the shopping trip. The girls tried on fancy outfits and told each other that they looked great. Tracey and Angelique bought the most and bragged about how much spending money they had.

"What do you think?" Angelique showed off her new silver watch to Tracey.

"Gorgeous, I need some jewelry too." Tracey declared.

She demanded we all follow her to the jewelry store on the second floor of the large shopping center. She pulled out a large wad of cash and made sure the bills were visible to all.

I looked at the diamond rings in the display cases and thought about the promise rings that some of the girls at my school wore. Their boyfriends gave them rings as a symbol of commitment. I longed for the day that I would receive a promise ring or even a silver bracelet. I paid close attention to the sterling silver shiny ones in the case.

"Mac!" Tracey boomed.

I snapped out of my fantasy.

"What?" I replied.

"It's time to go...I got my bracelet." She revealed a silver link chain on her thin brown wrist.

"Are you daydreaming about the jewels that you can't afford?" she asked.

"No...I-I was just thinking." I did not like her putting me on the spot.

The gentle mannered man behind the counter looked at me with kind eyes. "Would you like to try on a bracelet too?"

I was about to answer him when Tracey gave a flip of her hand, letting her new bracelet jingle.

"Mac has no money!" she informed the man.

I cringed inside.

"Oh..." he said, looking like he felt bad for me. Then, he met my gaze. "It does not cost any money to try on a piece of jewelry."

"We don't have time for this," Tracey interrupted. "I want to buy some new eye shadow!"

I refused to try on the bracelet because of the menacing looks I was gathering from the girls.

They all held tight to the large shopping bags with pretty handles that branded their favorite stores and added value to their identity. I just carried my purse, which was penniless and heavy with a novel and my sketch pad. My feet ached from walking around the crowded mall. I mostly walked along side Lara, because everyone else realized that being associated with me would make them look worse. I was relieved when we finally left the mall.

The bus pulled up to the amusement park with a screech. I sat by myself in the first seat on the fancy coach shuttle. The other girls chatted and gossiped about the boys they liked and what they bought at the mall. I settled into the warm seat's soft cushion. I tried to take comfort in the smell of the leather. I heard my name in so many sentences coming from the back of the bus.

"She is such a loser...Big Mac is a mess!" said a girl I did not even know.

They scurried off of the bus with determination when the driver announced that we could exit. I was the last one off, and I walked with Lara the whole time.

Lara directed us to a concession stand, where she bought herself a corn dog and a cup of hazelnut coffee. I thought that was a weird combination.

"Mackenzie, you want something?" she asked gulping down a hot sip of brown liquid.

My stomach rumbled angrily and wanted everything. The smell of fresh buttered popcorn mixed with steak fries filled my nostrils. I really wondered about the taste of the candy apples as I saw the other girls take large, enthusiastic bites of theirs. I smiled at Lara and told her thank you.

"I'm not really hungry," I said, feeling bad for lying.

Lara looked at me quizzically.

"Are you sure?"

"Yeah, I had a very big breakfast at the nook this morning," I said, recalling my feast on the silver plated tray.

I did not want Lara to have to pay for me. I did not think that was fair. I would be sure to have a bacon double cheeseburger when I got back to the camp grounds. I was happy when the bus driver told us to get back on the bus. It was the first time that I had been at an amusement park and did not get on a roller coaster. I heard the girls on the bus call me a poor loser, and I felt nausea well up in my belly. I was not sure if the stomach issues were because of my hunger or my sadness.

I hurried off the bus when we got back to Camp Ellington, and I raced for the grill. I was excited about drowning my sorrows in a juicy burger and salty french fries. My mouth watered, anticipating the taste of grease that would soothe away the stress of the day. When I saw the grill had closed ten minutes before I got there, I felt like someone had hit me with a hammer. I accepted the fact that I would have to eat cereal and milk, and raced into my living quarters, dropping my purse on the ground and heading for the answer to my hunger. I ransacked my mini fridge and discovered that my milk was gone. I stared at the empty carton with regret. I shook it hoping that my eyes were playing tricks on me.

I finally gave up and ate dry cereal by the handful, bypassing the bowl and spoon. I stared at the girl in the reflection in front of me and felt very sorry for her. The sweet crumbs stayed glued to her skin, and her brown eyes had a defeated look. Hot tears were ready to spill onto her cheeks, when a sharp knock on the door interrupted.

Lara had a Styrofoam container stuffed with a cheeseburger and french fries. The smell made my stomach rumble and my mouth water.

"Hey kid, I noticed you went to the grill after we were off of the bus, and they were closed," she started. "I needed coffee anyway, so I asked Madge if she had any food left and she wrapped this up for you." Lara handed me the package.

"Thanks," I said, excited to eat a meal of my favorites.

"Well, no problem," Lara mumbled. "I needed to grab some coffee anyway." She held up the paper cup of coffee in her other hand.

I smiled as Lara left the room. As I enjoyed my fast food meal, I looked back at the brown eyes in the mirror and saw a glimmer of hope in the reflection.

Chapter 10

In the last week of summer camp, Lara informed us that we would be having a picnic and an end of the season dance with the boys camp. I was excited about the picnic, but the dance seemed a little much.

First of all, I can't dance very well. This is one of the categories that I am not gifted in at all. Most of the girls at camp had formal training since they were three, and they always wanted to show off some new move they learned in their hip hop classes. I never took hip hop, or anything else, for that matter. I also never thought that I would go to a dance.

We had a formal at school once, but I did not go. No one asked me, and I stayed at home and watched movies with my mom. We made it a girls' night. My mom loves the same types of movies as me even though she's old, so we have a blast in our pajamas and head scarves (so that our hair styles stay pretty).

Zach called me later that day to see what I was up to. I was hoping that he'd ask me to the dance. We talked about soccer, drawing and the picnic, but he never brought up the dance. I was sad when we got off of the phone, because he never mentioned it. I wondered if he asked one of the other girls.

I looked in the mirror thoughtfully.

"Would I ask myself to the dance?" I thought aloud.

A face with scruffy brows and surrounded by lots of hair stared back at me. Zach was so nice, and I did not want to be too mushy, but I really wanted him to be my first dance date.

Technically, I am not allowed to date yet, but this was camp. It would be okay. I turned off the light on the vanity table and flopped down on my cushy bed. I hope he asks me, I prayed silently, until I drifted off to sleep.

Chapter 11

The Breakfast Nook was bustling with chatter when I got there the next morning. Girls were talking about their dates and the end of season dance. I listened closely to see if any of the girls mentioned Zach. Angelique was bragging about the note she received from a boy who wanted her to be his date.

"He gave me flowers and everything," she bragged.

"My date asked me in person," Tracey smiled.

"He actually said that he was happy to ask a beauty queen to the dance." She subtly tried to top Angelique's story.

Tracey looked at me with her new glitter eye shadow and braids.

"Are you going to the dance with anyone, Big Mac?" she asked cheerfully.

I took a deep breath out and slowly said,

"Tracey, I have to tell you, I hate it when you call me Big Mac."

Tracey looked shocked, and the smile went away from her face.

"I always call you that!" she argued. "All of the girls do. Why is it such a big deal now?"

Angelique butted in.

"Yeah, Mac. That's your name, remember?" She narrowed her pale blue eyes in my direction.

I took in another deep breath and realized that no tears were coming. This made me smile, a large smile like Tracey's.

"I don't know why I let you all treat me that way." My voice was steady, and I continued.

"My name is Mackenzie; I have two great parents that named me that."

I was sure to keep my head up and my voice even.

"If you don't like it, please don't talk to me."

I exhaled.

"If you call me Mac again, I will not answer you."

I continued to smile and ate my scrambled eggs. The table was silent and in utter shock.

"Mackenzie, I'm sorry that I laughed when people made fun of you," confessed a thin, short girl named Valentina, who has freckles and fire engine red hair. "I was afraid that if I defended you, they would make fun of me," she stated with confidence.

Her green eyes made contact with my brown eyes, and I saw that she was sincere. "Everyone at my school teases me and camp is the only place where I'm popular."

She was not laughing or smirking, and she had tears in her eyes. I gave her a wink and said,

"It's okay Valentina." I smiled. "Thanks for saying you are sorry."

"Well I'm not sorry," said Tracey, who had crossed her arms over her designer t-shirt. "I've been nothing but nice to you since you came here." She twisted her head, and her braids flew all over the place. "You are extremely lucky that you get to even be here!"

"I AM NOT LUCKY!" I said, in a voice so big, it surprised me. "Listen Tracey, I am smart and talented and that is why I won a scholarship and I do not feel bad about it."

"Luck had nothing to do with it," I added, with authority.

My sugary sweet smile could have given Tracey herself a tooth ache. Her smooth, brown face froze and for once, she was speechless. She looked at me as though I had slapped her in her face.

Lara came over quickly, looking embarrassed and exhausted. She held tight to her coffee mug.

"Girls, why are you all screaming?" she asked, looking nervous. "Is everything alright?"

I stepped toward her.

"Actually, I need to speak with you privately, Lara."

"Sure, Mackenzie," she said, taking a sip from her travel mug. We walked away from the girls at the table.

"Lara, my hair is a bit different from your hair, and when I get it wet, it is harder for me to style it," I said, respectfully.

"I am not trying to be shallow, but it would help me if you understood why I asked to be excused from the pool the other day." I watched her green eyes go wide with surprise.

Lara took another sip from her coffee mug and slowly smiled.

"Well Mackenzie, that was very mature of you to take me to the side and tell me that," she admitted.

"Thanks," I said.

She looked thoughtful and said, "I guess I was a bit hard on you." She giggled nervously.

"Now let's get going, because you are holding up the schedule with this chat!"

She put her arm around me, and we both laughed.

Chapter 12

I SIGNED UP ON the volunteer list to help decorate the camp ballroom for the dance. I found myself getting a good workout, climbing up and down the ladder to add streamers and balloons to the walls and ceiling.

"Wow…so nice of you to help out," Tracey said. She stood with her arms crossed, staring at my attempts to make the room more youthful.

"Thanks," I said, trying to assume the best of her intentions.

"If I did not have a date for the dance, I would not be so generous," she offered.

I sucked in my breath and decided that I would not let Tracey get to me. I ignored her last comment and continued to focus on the balloon I had just filled with helium.

Tracey waited around for me to react to her comments.

I continued to focus on the pretty balloons.

"Mackenzie, did you know that I was asked to the dance on the first day that it was announced?" she taunted in a polite voice.

I climbed off of the ladder, letting the balloon in my hand drift up to the ceiling. I realized that if I tried to ignore Tracey, she would not go away. I looked straight into her light brown eyes and said, "Tracey, you are such a pretty girl, but your attitude does not match." My tone was even and focused.

Her hands immediately went to her shiny black braids, and she caressed them out of habit.

"Are you jealous, Mackenzie?" she asked with a frown.

"Not at all," I said. "I just wonder why you go out of your way to be mean."

For the first time since I met Tracey, she looked defeated. She walked away quickly, her heels clicking on the wooden floor of the ballroom. I shrugged and went back to decorating. I smiled to myself and felt proud that I did not let her continue to tease me.

Lara thanked the volunteers for their help and told us that we were free to do what we wanted for the rest of the day. She mentioned that a movie was showing in the theater, if anyone wanted to go. I gathered my purse and was ready to walk back to my living quarters alone.

"Are you walking back to your quarters or are you going to the movie?" I heard a small voice ask.

I turned around and saw Valentina Smith. I shrugged my shoulders and told her that I was going to walk back.

"If you want, I can walk back with you. Or you can join me for the movie, if you want to have a friend to watch it with." She smiled.

"I think I'll watch the movie with you," I decided.

I felt light as a feather as me and Valentina laughed at the silly comedy that played on the big screen. We gobbled down large handfuls of buttered popcorn and drank cola.

After the movie, we walked back to the living quarters area, and we chatted about camp and the upcoming dance.

"I overheard you talking to Tracey," she stated. "It's cool that you stood up for yourself." She smiled.

"Thanks," I said.

I walked into my living quarters and noticed a white envelope on my floor.

I opened it and read:

"Mackenzie,

I know that I am not the nicest girl at camp.

I should not have given you problems about the dance and your tennis game.

I hate saying that I am sorry so I won't ...but I should not have been so mean.

Yours Truly,

Tracey Blake

I have to admit, that was probably one of the hardest things for Tracey to write. I pictured her looking tortured, writing the note while grabbing one of her extra long braids for extra strength. I appreciated her effort and felt that, even though she did not say that she was sorry for her cruelty, she was sorry. I folded the letter back up and looked in my mirror. The girl in front of me was changing into a new person, and I thought, "I like her."

Chapter 13

I walked around the end of season picnic with Valentina. She was really nice, now that I was getting to know her. She told me that, when she was at school, people made fun of her all of the time because of her freckles and bright hair color. We ate grilled burgers and played games.

The boys' bus pulled up, and I held my breath thinking about Zach. He never asked me to the dance. He had been calling me every night to chat about sports and stuff, but he always ended our talks without mentioning the dance.

All of the girls in my group had dates, even Valentina. She told me how Chase Sullivan, one of the cutest boys at camp, asked her to the dance. Her voice was filled with warmth as she revealed to me that this would be her first dance. It was nice to know that I was not the only one who thought camp could bring a new beginning and take away some of the negativity of school life.

The boys eagerly ran down the stairs of the shuttle bus and right for the food lines. They quickly filled their plates with burgers, hot dogs, chips and huge slices of cake. I'm not sure if they even noticed the fresh fruit and salad bar lines. Zach was the last one off of the bus and instead of going to the food lines like the other boys, he immediately walked over to me.

Valentina and I smiled at each other. I already told her that I thought I had a crush on him. She smiled and said hi to Zach, then she excused herself and went off to get a piece of pound cake.

Zach looked at me with his hazel eyes.

"So...Mackenzie."

I smiled.

"So....Zach."

He looked sad and stared at the grass on the ground. He cleared his throat and looked slightly uncomfortable.

"Are you going to the dance with someone already?"

I shook my head.

"No," I replied.

I looked at him with my heart beating so fast I was sure he would hear it. A grin spread across his brown face.

"Go with me!" he smiled.

"Okay," I said smiling back.

He took a deep breath and looked relieved.

"I was so nervous and afraid that you already had a date for the dance," he admitted.

"You are my best friend here, and you are so pretty with your awesome curly hair and sweet smile." I was shocked.

"Really?" I asked.

It felt magical as Zach confided in me.

"Yeah. I thought you would tell me no, so I never asked you and then I thought, I have to do it now or never." His smile broke into a wide grin.

"All of the guys here think that you are so great!" he admitted.

"They love how smart you are with your drawing pad and pretty smile."

I felt butterflies in my stomach.

I mustered up the courage to say what was on my mind. I sighed deeply and looked at him.

"I think that you are great," I said quietly.

Zach looked thrilled. We giggled softly and talked about soccer, drawing and now our dance as we walked around together.

The picnic was complete.

Tracey began to walk over to us. I caught her glance and willed her to stay away without saying anything. She cleared her throat and turned and walked in the other direction.

"I was afraid that she was going to come over here and tell me that you were on scholarship again," Zach laughed.

"Yeah, aren't we all?" I replied with confidence. We giggled and got in line to play horse shoes.

Chapter 14

I sat in my living quarters the night of the dance, opening a brightly colored package. Earlier that day, the cheery receptionist, Janice, handed me the small box and told me that I had to open it today before the dance. She smiled and happily rubbed her plump hands together.

"I hope it's something fun," she said with enthusiasm. Her cheeks blushed a perfect peach color.

I thanked her, accepting the mystery gift.

I carefully opened the box, trying not to tear the beautiful wrapping paper, so that I could recycle it. I removed beautiful layers of multicolored tissue paper to get to the beautiful gift inside. I gasped with delight as I looked at the delicate crystal object.

My parents sent me a crystal photo frame and a pastel colored note card that read:

Dearest Mackenzie,
You are the light of our life and we cannot wait for that light to be reflected in this picture frame.
Try and have the best time that you can tonight!
We wish that we could be there.
Since we can't, we were hoping that you could put a photo of you and your first date, Zach, inside of this frame and share it with us when you come home.
Have fun!
Love,
Mom & Dad :)

I immediately felt the warmth from my parent's thoughtfulness flood into my heart. I re-read the precious note two more times.

Finally, I placed the bright pink note card on my vanity table, and I realized that I felt better than I had in a long time. I took the pretty black party dress that I planned on wearing out of my borrowed faux leather suitcase. The dress was soft to the touch, and it felt like fine silk in my hands. I stared at it with sincere admiration for a while. I was going to my first dance with the cutest boy at camp. It was so funny to me that I once thought I would never have the need to unpack it.

After I was dressed for the dance, I looked in the large mirror and saw the confident girl staring back at me. She was so pretty. She had this great springy reddish-brown hair that curled perfectly and framed her face in ringlets without the need for a perm or added chemicals. Her smile was bright and beautiful, even with braces and an overbite, and she was smart and talented. Her smiling brown eyes held no tears anymore, only hope and anticipation for the future. I knew when it was time for me to return to school in Novingpond, I would be this new girl that I discovered at camp, not the timid girl who holds back her feelings and allows others to walk over her.

A sharp knock startled me.

"Mackenzie, don't hold us up," Lara yelled loudly through the closed door.

"You have five minutes to do what you need to!" She sounded exhausted.

"Okay!" I looked in the mirror and realized that I had less than five minutes to call my two best friends in the world.

I picked up the phone. I thought about Valentina and Zach.

"Hi Mom!" I said happily, bursting with enthusiasm.

"Hi Baby girl!" Her dazzling smile shined even through the phone.

"I'm going to grab your dad and have him get on the other phone," she said.

Yes, of course Zach and Valentina were my friends, but dorky as it might seem, Mom and Dad have always been there for me. Dad taught me how to fix a flat tire, and Mom taught me how to wrap up my hair so that it did not get messed up when I slept. What a combination! Seriously, true friends can't get any better than that.

LaVergne, TN USA
25 September 2010
198378LV00001B/5/P